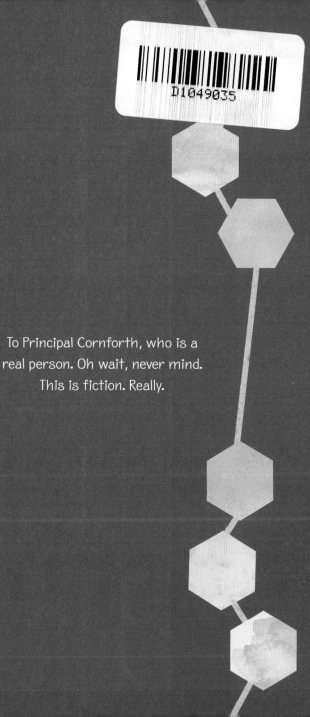

D1049035

To Principal Cornforth, who is a real person. Oh wait, never mind. This is fiction. Really.

The McCarthys

If families were pizzas, mine would be THE WORKS. We have a little bit of everything.

CURIOUS (age 10) Sauce – I like to hide in the background and avoid the spotlight.

ANNE (age 11) Pickles – She adds comic relief.

JOHN GLENN (age 8) Anchovies – He makes you pucker at the unexpected ingredient.

EDISON (age 4) Parmesan – He's the sprinkles, spilling off the pizza and onto the plate.

BENJAMIN (age 5) Pepperoni – He likes perfect circles. Spread equally around the pizza.

MRS. STICKLER (age 103, I think) My fourth-grade teacher.

MS. FICKLEBY (age 203) An ancient reading teacher with some interesting "friends."

MR. CORNFORTH Principal and lover of fancy coffee drinks.

MR. MACK A cool fifth-grade teacher, who I have never met, and at this rate, I never will meet.

MR. GRUMPUS A loud librarian.

AUNT DOLLY A nurse who believes popsicles cure most things.

EMILY (age 12) Jalapeños – She always adds something exotic to our family. And she's weird.

CHARLOTTE (age 13) Crust – She bosses us around and keeps us inside the lines.

MOM Mozzarella cheese – When she reads to us at night, she is warm and gooey and holds us together.

DAD Dough – He provides lots of structure for all the messy toppings . . . or messy kids.

JESSE Kid from Ms. Fickleby's class. Just part of a chain reaction.

SOFIA A third-grade princess lover at Hilltop Elementary.

LIN TRAN Part of the fourth-grade cold-lunch crowd at Hilltop Elementary.

RANDY STUDLEY Peanut-butter-and-mayo sandwich lover.

HENRY WONG Another fourth grader at Hilltop Elementary.

ROBIN FINCH According to her mother, a very clever fourth grader at Hilltop Elementary.

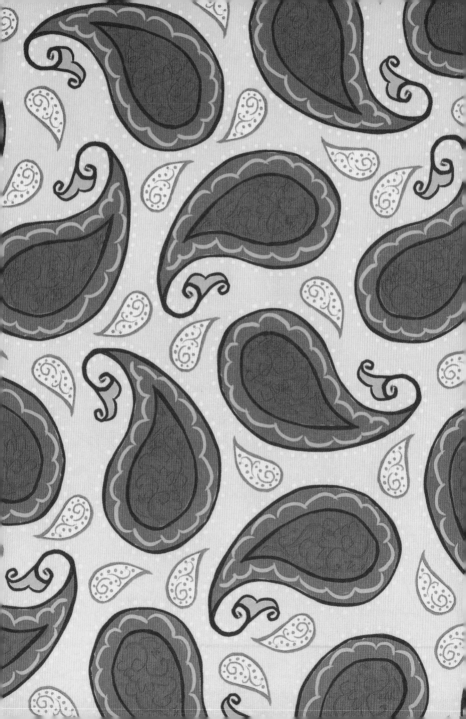

All happy families are *not* alike — especially families with seven kids. But happy families *are* a lot like pizzas. Once you find the right combination of ingredients, things go together nicely.

My name is Curious McCarthy. I am in the fourth grade, and I am going to be a scientist. I just recently decided on this career, so I am practicing. As a serious scientist, I use footnotes.[1]

And for the record, my family is pretty much a happy family . . . if you can ignore dirty socks on the sofa and long lines outside the bathroom. Big families can also be a lot of work. Even happy ones. It takes some experimentation to get things right.

Last week I decided to try chemistry. My week as a chemist went something like this . . .

---

1   Footnotes for a scientist are like spices for a chef — they aren't absolutely necessary, but they make life so much more interesting.

"How do I look?" Dad asked.

"Great," Mom said.

"Except for the white socks," said my oldest sister, Charlotte.

As a scientist, I like to observe. And tonight I observed something unusual. Dad was wearing a suit. He doesn't usually wear a suit.[2]

"You want to look professional for your week at B-Dale Engineering," Mom said.

That was it. Dad was going back to work. Dad is retired. So normally he stays at home. He usually does all the cooking and a lot of the cleaning and stuff. But sometimes he takes a temporary job for extra cash.

"You kids are going to start helping with dinner," Mom said, starting our family meeting.

Sunday night is family meeting night. In a family with seven kids, meetings are necessary for things

----

2   Scientists like to use footnotes to clarify information. And just to clarify, Dad usually wears jeans and a shirt with a pocket protector.

to run smoothly. Actually, meetings are necessary to avoid chaos.

Dad is an engineer. He is very organized. He makes precise meals. I was curious to hear how the kids would be helping.

"I have it all planned out," Dad said. He tacked a chart to the refrigerator. "The five oldest kids will cook dinner Monday through Friday. Mom and I will cover the weekend."

We were listed on the chart by age. The columns on Dad's chart looked something like this:

Day	Chief Cook	Menu	Team Helpers
Monday	Charlotte	Ratatouille & French Bread	Emily, Anne
Tuesday	Emily	Tacos & Dirty Rice	Anne, Curious
Wednesday	Anne	Vegetable Soup	Curious, John Glenn
Thursday	Curious	Hot Dogs & Lemonade	John Glenn, Benjamin
Friday	John Glenn	Homemade Pizza	Edison, Dad

Only Dad's chart had two more columns. In the fifth column he listed the ingredients. And finally, in column six, were the cookbook and page number.[3]

I studied the chart. Being the fourth child, I did not get to cook until Thursday. I couldn't wait to get in the kitchen and start brewing something up. Dad worked his kitchen counter like a chemist works his bench. I was hoping I would get to mix together some liquids and solids and create a chemical reaction.[4]

I would get to be a helper starting on Tuesday.

"Every good engineer," Dad began, "and scientist," he said looking at me, "has to learn to work with a team."

Looking at the chart, I wondered about the teams. I also wondered how the teams would work together.

---

3   Scientists use references in publications to give credit to other people for their ideas. But this is fiction. So I don't need references. Really.

4   A lot of cooking is really chemistry and involves a series of chemical reactions. For example, why do you think meat turns brown when you cook it? It has something to do with the breaking down of the bonds between protein molecules, but don't ask me. I am not a chemist yet!

Charlotte was chief cook on Monday. That was easy for Charlotte. She is used to being in charge. But what about the rest of the week when Charlotte is not in charge? I figured she was probably mad about that.

Then I looked a little closer at the chart. Charlotte was not a helper all week. I thought that was pretty clever of Dad. He probably knows that Charlotte could not be on a team without taking charge.

"I'll be home early on Friday to help John Glenn with the pizza. I have a new recipe!" Dad said.

Every adult in the world thinks John Glenn is an angel. Every adult in the world is wrong. John Glenn is trouble. So having Dad in the kitchen with John Glenn is a good idea. I hoped that Dad would remember to change out of his suit.

"And here is the list of chores for the week!" announced Dad. He put a second chart next to the first. Wednesdays were chore nights. But with Dad being gone all week, we would apparently have to do chores every day.

The second chart looked like this:

Daily Chores	Time	Responsible Party
Check homework and update calendars	4:15	Anne
Transport laundry to the laundry room	4:30	Benjamin
Fold napkins and set table	5:15	Edison
Wipe off table and load dishwasher	6:45	John Glenn
Sweep floors and vacuum carpets	7:00	Emily
Scrub the toilet	7:15	Charlotte

I studied the second chart. Something was missing.

Or some*one*. Dad had left me out. At first, it surprised

me that Dad would make a mistake and leave me

out. He is normally very organized. But maybe this

temporary job had him frazzled. It would *really*

surprise me if my three older sisters didn't notice.

But I wasn't going to say a word. I could use the extra

time to study how to be a chemist.

2

Sunday, 7:32 p.m.

Mom is an English professor and works long hours. She doesn't like to cook. The last time Dad took a temporary job, Mom bought a truckload of hot dogs, a green cake, and six bags of potato chips. It was fun at the beginning, but that stuff got old after a week.

Mom also doesn't like to do laundry. That is why there was a week's worth of socks piled on the table. She decided she would read to us while we matched socks. She read a book called *Original Recipe*.[5]

We matched socks for what seemed like hours.

Mom finished the book.

"Let's finish the socks quickly and get to bed early," Mom said.

---

5   *Original Recipe* is a book by Jessica Young. Mom was apparently trying to inspire great cooking during the next week.

She stared at the still-overwhelming pile of
unmatched socks. "One can never have enough
socks." She sighed.

"Anyone see the mate to this sock?" Dad asked.
He was holding up a very professional-looking
black sock.

"You should wear your Elmo socks!" suggested Emily. I have three older sisters. Emily is the second oldest. She is the first weirdest.

"How about these?" asked Charlotte, my oldest and perfectly perfect sister.

"Those are argyles!" said my sister Anne, rolling her eyes.[6]

"Those aren't *our* gyles! They're *my* gyles!" said Edison, my youngest brother.[7]

----

6   Argyles are socks with a pattern that looks kind of plaid. Like a kilt. A kilt is a man's skirt. Kilts come from Scotland, but we are Irish, and I am not really sure why we have argyles.

7   I have three younger brothers. John Glenn is the oldest, followed by Ben and Edison. John Glenn was named after an astronaut. Apparently Dad had high hopes for him. It is my observation that Dad should put his money on one of his other kids.

3

Monday, 8:00 a.m.

I trudged into school on Monday morning. I was not looking forward to seeing my teacher, Mrs. Stickler. She had it out for me.

As soon as we were all seated, Mrs. Stickler made an announcement. The fourth graders were now going to change classes for reading. Eventually, all the grades would be changing classes for reading.

Eight kids would go to Ms. Fickleby's class. Eight kids would go to Mr. Mack's class. Eight kids would stay with Mrs. Stickler.[8]

Ms. Fickleby is the third-grade teacher, and Mr. Mack is the fifth-grade teacher. It does not take a scientist to figure out where I was going.

---

8   I had to admire Mrs. Stickler's sense of equality. At least she was dividing us into equal parts.

Even with an English professor for a mom, I do not like to read. I am more of a hands-on kind of kid. Dad says I am a visual learner. That means I need to see stuff. I like to observe people and nature and other things. People and nature are more interesting than words on pages.

After lunch, the Unfortunate Eight lined up. We marched down the hall to Ms. Fickleby's class.

Ms. Fickleby is even more old-fashioned than Mrs. Stickler. And about a hundred years older.

I observed Ms. Fickleby. She wore a shawl. A shawl is like a knit blanket that hangs over someone's shoulders. No real modern people wear shawls. Ms. Fickleby is ancient. When we were all seated, she pulled out a book on Jimmy Carter. Really ancient.[9]

---

9   Jimmy Carter was the thirty-ninth president of the United States. That was a long, long, long time ago.

Ms. Fickleby explained how our reading group would work. She would read about one of her favorite subjects. We would follow along. Then we would each take turns reading a paragraph out loud. Oh, *great*.[10]

After that *wonderful* task, Ms. Fickleby said, "Now we will do some word exercises."

I imagined us bending our bodies into the shapes of letters. How was a 203-year-old teacher going to do that? Luckily for her, that is not what she had in mind.

We were going to make word sandwiches. Technically, a sandwich is some meat and cheese between two pieces of bread. Or it could be peanut butter and banana. Or if you are a creepy kid from the fourth grade named Randy Studley, it could be peanut butter and mayo. The key to a good sandwich is to combine the right mix of things you like.

But Ms. Fickleby's word sandwich is two words smashed together. Like *liger*, which is part *lion* and

---

10   This is sarcasm. It is when you say one thing, but mean the opposite. So reading a paragraph out loud is NOT great. It is cruel.

part *tiger*. I wondered why it wasn't a *tigon* — part *tiger* and part *lion*.[11]

This would be a good place for a chart. Scientists like charts. But Ms. Fickleby is not a scientist. While Ms. Fickleby made up more word sandwiches, I opened my notebook and started my own chart:

lion	+	tiger	=	liger
breakfast	+	lunch	=	brunch
smoke	+	fog	=	smog
guess	+	estimate	=	guesstimate

---

11   The real word for a word sandwich is *portmanteau* (you say it like three words smashed together: PORT-MAN-TOE), which is from a French word that really means suitcase and not sandwich. But *portmanteau* is too big of a word for third and fourth graders. I am sure you are wondering how anyone demoted to the third-grade reading group knows this. Poor readers are not *STUPID*, we just *like* to read slowly. I happen to know lots of big words. My mother is an English professor, remember?

The last one was not one of Ms. Fickleby's word sandwiches. I thought of that one myself. It seemed like a good word sandwich for a scientist.

Ms. Fickleby perplexified me.[12]

She loved her words. She loved her sentences. She loved her books. You could see it on her face. She was smiling at her words, sentences, and books all the time. How can anyone love words so much?

At the end of our reading hour, she handed out take-home packets. They held our reading assignments. She said, "Remember, class, books are your friends."

Books are your *friends*? This school has lots of strange ideas. I imagined Ms. Fickleby playing with her books after school. A little chuckle started, but I held it back and it turned into a snortle.[13]

----

12   Perplexed + Terrified = Perplexified. I just made up that word sandwich. It is a state of being both puzzled and a bit scared, the usual state of a fourth grader who is sent to the third-grade room for reading.

13   Snort + Chortle = Snortle. A snortle is a little piglet-like sound that occurs when you try to hold back a laugh. I just made that up. I am getting the hang of this word sandwich stuff.

4

Monday, 3:45 p.m.

Aunt Dolly was at the house when we got home.

She brought popsicles. She always brings popsicles.

She was there to watch my youngest brother,

Edison. "He's all yours now!" she said to Charlotte as

she rushed out the door. Apparently Aunt Dolly was

in a hurry.

Charlotte walked over to the chore chart. I inched

my way to the back of the crowd.

"Anne," said Charlotte, "start checking homework."

I slipped farther back. I wanted to slip away

unnoticed. Then maybe no one would see that I wasn't

assigned a chore. I was about one meter away from the

living-room door.[14]

---

14   I am a scientist. Scientists use SI units. The meter is an SI unit. SI stands for
the International System of Measurement. You might be wondering why they aren't
called the ISM units, but that is too complicated for a fourth grader. If you figure it out,
let me know.

My brothers and sisters grabbed popsicles.
I was tempted. But a popsicle was not worth getting
noticed.

My brothers moved toward the kitchen table.
Anne was digging through backpacks. Emily was
looking out the window. Charlotte was studying the
chore chart. I moved 2.54 centimeters closer to the
living-room door.[15]

---
15   Centimeters are also SI units. And 2.54 centimeters is about an inch. But I bet you
already know that because only the smartest kids read the footnotes.

"John Glenn," said Charlotte. "Wipe down the table. NOW! We don't want our homework to get sticky."

John Glenn sprayed Dad's homemade cleaner all over the table. He also sprayed it all over the chairs. He came close to spraying it all over Charlotte.[16]

I moved a little closer to the living-room door.

My brothers and sisters were settling around the table. Anne was lining up homework sheets.

Ben is in kindergarten. That means he doesn't get homework. I was just thinking about how easy kindergarten was when Charlotte picked up a basket.

"Ben, go collect laundry," said Charlotte.

Maybe being a kindergartner isn't that great after all.

As Charlotte was handing the basket to Ben, I quickly slipped around the corner.

----

16   I am sure you are wondering why Dad makes his own cleaner. It is thrifty. That means that it is cheap. And big families need to be thrifty. The cleaner is made from water and vinegar. Vinegar is an acid, which makes it good for killing some germs. Don't worry, it won't kill Charlotte.

"Curious!" shouted Charlotte. "Get back in here!"

Bummer. She must have noticed that I was not assigned a chore. But she said, "Anne, make sure you check Curious's homework first. She was trying to get away."[17]

---

17   For the record, I was not trying to get away from having my homework checked, but that is not a bad idea either.

5

Monday, 4:45 p.m.

Our homework session was over, so I grabbed my library books.

Tuesday is library day. My books had to be returned, and I hadn't even read them. I did not want to miss any interesting facts, especially facts that might be related to chemistry. So I scanned the pages while I waited for the cooking to start.

"Go wash your hands and face," Charlotte said to Edison.

"Why?" said Edison.

"Because you are a drippy, popsicle mess," said Charlotte. I looked up from my book. Charlotte was right. He *was* a drippy, popsicle mess.

"So?" said Edison.

"So, you can't set the table with sticky hands!" she replied. "No one wants your germs on their forks and knives."

"Edison and I aren't allowed to touch knives," Ben said.

Seeing that she would not get anywhere with Edison, Charlotte said, "John Glenn, take the boys to your room. Stay there so I can get dinner ready."

The boys grabbed more popsicles and slipped up the back stairs.

I wanted to tell her that leaving John Glenn in charge was a problem.[18]

I kept my mouth shut. I did not want to get sent away. I wanted to stay. I wanted to study the cooking process. I couldn't wait to see what chemistry might happen.

Scientists like to make a hypothesis now and then. A hypothesis is an educated guess. Here's mine . . .

---

18 Defining your problem is the very first step you should take when you follow the scientific method. Apparently, Charlotte is not a scientist. She did not see the problem.

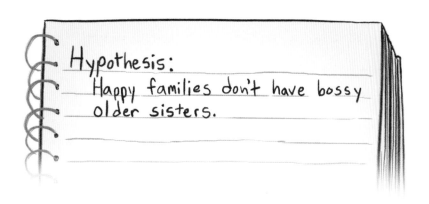

Hypothesis:
Happy families don't have bossy older sisters.

I thought about my guess. I wondered if Charlotte would be as bossy with Emily and Anne as she is with the rest of us.

Charlotte took some vegetables out of the refrigerator. "Time to start the ratatouille," she said.

We always eat meatless on Mondays. Some scientists think that eating meatless is environmentally responsible. And some scientists think eating more vegetables is good for your health.

Dad might believe these things too. But the fact is, the McCarthys eat meatless because it is cheap. And as I mentioned before, with seven kids, my parents have to spend wisely.

"RAT-A-TOO-EEEEEE!" Emily sang. Emily doesn't speak French, but she loves to say exotic words. She takes Spanish at the middle school. She does not take French. Her way of helping was to shout each ingredient in another language.

"RAT-AH-TOO-EEEEEE is French for rat food!" said Emily.

Ratatouille is actually a French dish made with stewed vegetables. All mushed up. No wonder they named it after a rat. Technically, that is incorrect. But I am sure Emily is not the first to understand its double meaning.[19]

"What's a rat's favorite game?" asked Anne.

Charlotte stared at her.

"Hide-and-squeak!" Anne laughed. Emily laughed too. Charlotte did not laugh.

At least part of this team was having fun. It seemed like the only chemistry I was going to observe tonight was family chemistry.[20]

----

19   The word *ratatouille* really has nothing to do with rats. It comes from two French words: *ratouiller* and *tatouiller*. Don't try to pronounce these. They are forms of the French verb *touiller*, which means "to stir up." As in stirring up tomatoes, zucchini, onions, eggplant, and peppers. Apparently Charlotte will be stirring up dinner, while John Glenn, Ben, and Edison are stirring up trouble.

20   I am not sure if family chemistry is a real thing. But I suppose it is like when a team works well together. Or kind of like a performance – everyone plays a role. Charlotte's role is chief cook. Emily's role is translator. That is someone who tells you what words mean in a different language. Anne's role is comedian.

6

Monday, 5:49 p.m.

Charlotte was stirring the ratatouille when Dad walked in. Dad took a deep sniff. He smiled. "It smells great in here!" he said to Charlotte. She smiled.

Mom walked in balancing a stack of books. I observed *In the Night Kitchen* on the top of the pile. Mom reads out loud to us every night. Knowing Mom, she probably had a good reason for reading *In the Night Kitchen*. Mom took a whiff, and she smiled too.

We scrambled like rats around the table. It is an old library table, and it has drawers underneath. They were probably meant for papers and writing utensils.

John Glenn has a history of sneaking strange foods into the drawers. Sometimes he slips a little of his dinner under the table for the dog.[21]

---

21   We don't have a dog.

As we all helped ourselves to a portion of rat food, I made some observations.[22]

Dad took a large portion. Mom took a large portion. Charlotte, Emily, and Anne took medium-sized portions. The rest of us took the smallest portions we could get away with.

I studied my portion.

It was not really a solid and not really a liquid. It was somewhere in between. I am not sure what scientists call that.

This is the right time for a word sandwich. I am going to call it a *sliquid*. We had to eat our sliquid with sporks.[23]

Tonight I observed that John Glenn was sitting in Charlotte's usual spot. As Mom and Dad were enjoying their first taste of sliquid, John Glenn made a move.

---

22   A portion is how you divide something that is whole. Like one slice of pizza would be one portion of a whole pizza. Speaking of pizza, I wish we were having pizza.

23   Spoon + Fork = Spork. This is a useful utensil that keeps the drippy vegetables from sliding back onto the plate. Aren't we lucky?

He opened Charlotte's drawer and slid the sliquid off his plate and into the drawer. Charlotte would have a nice surprise someday soon.[24]

Mom and Dad enjoyed the ratlike dish. They nodded and smiled as they ate. I had to admit, it wasn't half bad. Even if it was a sliquid.

"This is delicious!" said Mom, giving Charlotte a look of approval. Although Charlotte was no scientist, dinner was prepared exactly to plan. Precise.

When dinner was over, Dad walked over to the chore chart. "Now, let's see," he said. "John Glenn, you can start loading the dishwasher. Anne can help." He winked at Anne.

Dad would have the family running smoothly in no time. "Emily," Dad said, "you can sweep when John Glenn is done . . . and Charlotte, the toilet is ready when you are!"

----

24   Remember sarcasm? Obviously, this will *not* be a nice surprise for Charlotte. Last week, Dad nailed all the drawers shut, so John Glenn could not slip any of his unwanted food inside. Except that Dad missed Charlotte's drawer, which *was* a nice surprise for John Glenn.

We all laughed. All of us, that is, except Charlotte.

She smiled sweetly when Dad handed her the
toilet brush and more of his homemade cleaner. But
when she turned to leave the room, she glared right
at me. A scientist might conclude that Charlotte
knew I didn't have a chore. I felt a tiny bit guilty.
But scientists need to spend time doing science,
not chores.

Tuesday, 1:15 p.m.

We sat in reading class the next day. Ms. Fickleby clucked her tongue and said, "Be kind to your books."

I remembered yesterday when she talked about books as friends. I wondered if she learned her clucking from her friend *The Little Red Hen*.

We had to miss library day. I guess with the new reading groups they just couldn't get the schedule worked out. We even had snack time with our reading class instead of homeroom. They should hire my dad.

I munched on my peanut-butter crackers. I reached into my backpack. Suddenly Ms. Fickleby cried, "Curious!" She didn't seem mad. Just alarmed.

"Remember, class, books are your friends. Don't handle them with sticky fingers," she said kindly.

"That is a very important book rule. You can have your snack. You can read a book. But don't do both at the same time!"

We snacked for about 2.3 minutes. Then Ms. Fickleby said, "Put your snacks away."

I looked at my fingers. They were a little sticky. Ms. Fickleby probably eats her peanut-butter crackers with a fork and knife. Or maybe a spork. I stopped eating and wiped my hands on my jeans.

It was book report time. Since I had only been in Ms. Fickleby's reading class for two days, I did not have to do a book report. That is a good thing, since we already know that books are *NOT* my friends.

The girl who sat in front of me, a third grader named Sofia, shared a book.

It was about a princess academy. The curled and worn pages alarmed Ms. Fickleby.

"Remember, class, use a bookmark and don't fold pages. Books are your friends," said Ms. Fickleby. She had as many rules as friends.

I decided to track these rules on a chart in my notebook. I made a column for my own rules too.

Sofia smoothed out her page, and Ms. Fickleby's worried face smoothed over with a romantical look.[25]

---

25 *Romantical* is a word sandwich. Romantic + Impractical = Romantical. It is a dreamy condition, common in princesses, frogs, and elderly third-grade reading teachers. And yes, I made it up.

Ms. Fickleby's Book Rules	Curious McCarthy's Book Rules
① Don't handle books with sticky fingers!	① Pick any book. Even nonfiction!
② Don't fold pages!	② You can read with a snack!
③ Don't leave your books outside!	③ Skip pages or whole chapters!
④ Don't let toddlers touch your books!	④ Read on the floor or outside!
⑤ Don't read in the bathtub!	⑤ You can read any way you want, even upside down!

She was probably imagining that she was at the princess academy. Maybe she was sharing dinner with Prince Charming. I wondered if characters like Snow White and Cinderella were her friends too.

I continued to study Ms. Fickleby. I imagined her having tea with Little Miss Muffet. But she wouldn't have curds and whey.[26]

I switched from observing Ms. Fickleby to observing student behavior. I studied the room. My notebook was ready, just in case I saw anything useful to write down. Or if Ms. Fickleby announced more book rules.

I snuck the rest of my peanut-butter crackers from my backpack and set them on my lap. I munched on them as I continued to study the room.

I watched Randy Studley and Henry Wong. Henry had something in his hand. Randy tried to grab it.

---

26   Just for your information, curds and whey is like cottage cheese. It is chemically complex. It is made of milk. Milk has dozens of proteins floating around in it. Cottage-cheese makers separate the proteins into clumps (curds) and liquid (whey). This chemical mixture would be too messy for Ms. Fickleby.

They started pushing each other. I thought I saw them puffing up their chests.[27]

Fortunately for Randy and Henry, Ms. Fickleby is not a good observer. She is not a scientist.

Ms. Fickleby said, "Line up, ladies and gentlemen! It's time to go back to homeroom."

---

27   This behavior is also common in primates, which are apes and chimpanzees. Their behavior is similar to behavior of the boys in this class.

"Ladies and gentlemen, LINE UP!" she sang.
I dropped my peanut-butter crackers all over the
floor. This startled Jesse, who dropped his book,
which crashed right on top of some peanut-butter
crackers. The crashing book startled Sofia, who
knocked over my milk — which I had forgotten on my
desk. The milk flew across the room, splattering the
books on Ms. Fickleby's desk.

The whole thing was one big chain reaction.[28]

"Curious McCarthy!" Ms. Fickleby cried in a panic. She was probably worried about her special friends.

As the rest of the Unfortunate Eight walked back to homeroom, I walked straight to the principal's office.

Ms. Fickleby trailed closely behind, saying, "Please be more careful, dear. We do not handle books with sticky fingers! Books are your friends."

As I passed the plastic chairs outside the principal's office, I noticed John Glenn sitting there, waiting his turn. Ms. Fickleby ignored the waiting kids and led me right in.

I glanced around as Ms. Fickleby chattered away to Principal Cornforth on the importance of keeping books safe and dry.

----

28   A chain reaction is when you have a series of events where each event triggers the next. It's like knocking over one domino and having a whole row of them fall over. Except replace that first domino with a peanut-butter cracker and . . . you get the idea.

Finally she turned and left. She was probably going to put life jackets on her closest companions.[29]

Principal Cornforth called me to his desk. He swallowed the last bite of his egg-salad sandwich.[30]

He was about to fold the corner of a page in his book, when I yelled, "STOP! Books are your friends!"

This would have been all right if it hadn't startled him. He spilled his caramel latté all over his desk.

I spent the next fifteen minutes helping Principal Cornforth clean up his office. Without any help from Snow White or Cinderella.

---

29   Companion is another word for friend. In Ms. Fickleby's case they are probably the butcher, the baker, and the candlestick maker – they would need life jackets before they all went out to sea.

30   Egg salad in this case is not a reference to Humpty Dumpty, although Humpty Dumpty is probably one of Ms. Fickleby's friends too.

8

Tuesday, 3:35 p.m.

When we got home from school, Aunt Dolly made her usual quick exit and left Charlotte in charge.

Anne went to work on the backpacks.

Emily started coloring with Edison.

John Glenn and Ben started heading for the back stairs.

"Ben! Laundry!" Charlotte ordered as she handed him the laundry basket.[31]

I learned my lesson yesterday. I was not going to try to slip away. Instead, I sat nervously at the table. I grabbed a purple crayon and started scribbling with Emily and Edison. I waited patiently for Anne's homework check.

----

31   You're probably wondering why Ben has to gather laundry every single day. Well, if you had a family of nine, you would be doing a load every day too. Or your mom would. Or your dad. Or if you're lucky, it would be the housekeeper.

I glanced at Charlotte as she stood at the refrigerator. She was studying Dad's charts again. She walked over to the table and glared at me.

"No trying to get out of your homework today, Curious!" she said.

I stared at her in amazement. I thought for sure she had noticed my missing name. But maybe she hadn't noticed.

I quickly opened my reading packet. I pulled out the book *Rapunzel: Her Princess Journal*. Great. I get to read about one of Ms. Fickleby's friends.

Charlotte must have noticed my disappointment.

"If you don't like that book, Curious, you can read mine." Charlotte smiled. Then she pulled her book out of her backpack. *Gift of Peace: The Jimmy Carter Story*. Great — another of Ms. Fickleby's friends.

9

Tuesday, 4:26 p.m.

Charlotte is good about bossing people around. But this was Emily's day to cook. It was Taco Tuesday.

Since Charlotte wasn't part of the team today, I would have to make a new hypothesis.

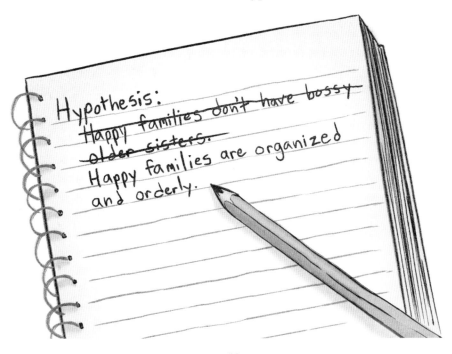

Hypothesis:
~~Happy families don't have bossy older sisters.~~
Happy families are organized and orderly.

Emily put on Mom's frilly apron. She called to Anne, "Get me the LAY-CHOOO-GAH!"

Anne went to the refrigerator and grabbed a head of lettuce.[32]

Emily is no engineer like Dad. She is not organized. I knew from observing Dad in the past that Emily should have cooked the meat before shredding lettuce.

"Get me the CAR-NAY!" Emily said. She must have been reading my mind. She was weird that way. I went to the refrigerator and grabbed the ground beef.

"Get me the TOE-MAH-TAYS!" shouted Emily. Anne grabbed the tomatoes.

Anne and I shredded lettuce, while Emily grabbed a pan to brown the beef.

"I'll do that," ordered Charlotte. "You are not allowed to operate the stove."

---

32   *Lechuga* is the Spanish word for lettuce. This is a word that every McCarthy knows. That is because Emily sings it every time lettuce is served. Emily is weird.

This is not true. Emily can use the stove.

But Emily is too smart to argue with Charlotte.

This wasn't even Charlotte's day to be in the
kitchen. I guess it takes all kinds of people to form
a good team. Or a happy family. Even bossy sisters.
Charlotte controlled everything when Mom and Dad
weren't around.

I decided to observe the solids, liquids, and gases involved in making dinner. Meat, lettuce, and cheese all appeared to be solids. The tomatoes could get sliquiddy.

Especially if you cooked them.

Or combined them with the meat.

That is what Dad would do. Dad is efficient. Emily is not efficient. She did not combine the meat and tomatoes. That is a good thing, especially for Ben. He does not like his foods to touch.

My mind wandered to Ms. Fickleby. I wondered if she and Rapunzel were taking turns doing each other's hair. Getting ready for book club. I snortled, which caused Charlotte to look over.

This is called cause and effect. And getting Charlotte's attention was not the effect I wanted. I needed to be silent and not influence the experiment. I also needed to be silent so Charlotte would forget about me. And forget about my chorelessness.

I stopped snortling.

10

Tuesday, 5:47 p.m.

"Let's do a cafeteria line," Anne suggested.[33] I was impressed with Anne's suggestion. A line would be more efficient than passing around toppings.

Mom and Dad walked in and saw us all lined up.

"Let's start!" said Dad. We rushed through the cafeteria line. Actually, it was more of a curve than a line. And it was a bit frenzied. But we all made it through in one piece . . . only a few taco shells were hurt in the process.

Eating never takes long on Taco Tuesday. When we were finished, I managed to slip away from the table before anyone could look at the chore chart.

But a little while later I came out of the bathroom and Charlotte was standing there.

---
33   Anne is going to be a great teacher someday. Or a great lunch lady.

She had the toilet brush in one hand and the spray in the other. She was wearing rubber gloves.

She shook the toilet brush at me and grinned. She must have noticed that I didn't have a chore. I started to feel a little bad about that. But not bad enough to scrub a toilet. I rushed past her and up the stairs.

11

Wednesday, 1:14 p.m.

Mrs. Stickler announced that we were going to have library time with our reading classes. Not with our homeroom classes. A different schedule again. They *really* need to hire my dad. He'd get this schedule worked out in no time flat. He'd even make a chart.

When the time came, the Unfortunate Eight headed down to Ms. Fickleby's class.

We started our daily word exercises. Ms. Fickleby gave us more word sandwiches. This got me to thinking about solids and liquids. When you combine a solid and a liquid or a solid and a solid, it can become something different. Like two words can become something different. Like a lion and a tiger can become a liger.

I decided it was another good time for a chart.

I opened my notebook and started recording:

Soil + water = mud
water + flour = pizza dough
water + sugar + yeast = lemonade
water + vinegar + lemons = Dad's homemade cleaner

"Curious?" said Ms. Fickleby. "Are you listening?"

"Yes, Ms. Fickleby," I said in my sweetest voice.

I was on my best behavior.[34]

After twelve minutes of word sandwiches, it was library time.

We walked to the library.

---

34   Well not really, but at least I could *sound* like I was on my best behavior.

I looked through the nonfiction section. I found a book on chemistry called *Mixtures and Solutions.* I sat down on the floor and began to study the pictures. I learned that a liquid takes the shape of its container. That is obvious. I pulled out another book called *Edible Chemicals.* That sounded interesting.

I grabbed another book called *Cool Chemistry Concoctions*. There were pictures of tie-dyed shirts and alien masks. The masks were made of a liquid that turned into a solid. One of the masks in the book looked a little like Mr. Grumpus, our librarian. Now that's cool chemistry.

"Time to check out your books!" called Mr. Grumpus. Apparently, the rule that says you have to be quiet in the library does not apply to the librarian.

I checked out *Edible Chemicals* and *Cool Chemistry Concoctions*. Then I headed back to homeroom to pick up my lunch bag.

A little while later I sat at the cold-lunch table. Lin Tran and Robin Finch sat across from me. I really wished that I could have had hot lunch. It was pizza day.

"My mother says that cold lunch is more nutritious," Robin said.

Lin smiled at her.

"But pizza has all the food groups," I said.

"Food groups aren't everything," answered Robin. "My mother says school pizza is too greasy."

"I like greasy pizza," I said.

Robin shook her head. "You really are curious," she said.

I ignored Robin and thought about pizza.

I would like a nice greasy pizza with pepperoni and black olives.

I opened my lunch bag. I pulled out a sandwich. The real kind of sandwich. Not a word sandwich.

Dad must have been in a hurry when he made lunches. My sandwich was out of equilibrium.[35]

---

35 Equilibrium is when something is balanced. My sandwich was OUT of equilibrium because there was much more peanut butter than jelly.

12

Wednesday is our regular chore night. It was time for

a new hypothesis:

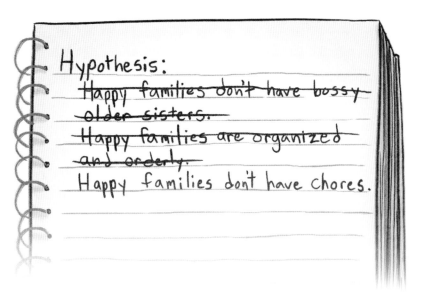

Hypothesis:
~~Happy families don't have bossy older sisters.~~
~~Happy families are organized and orderly.~~
Happy families don't have chores.

On most Wednesdays, we do chores after dinner.

So Charlotte decided we should get the afternoon off.

Well, not *off* exactly. We just got to skip chores and do homework instead.

Normally, I would rather do chores than homework. But I wasn't about to complain. That would get me noticed. I wanted to stay invisible so I could study more chemistry. At least I wanted to stay invisible to Charlotte, who was studying the two charts on the refrigerator.

I opened *Cool Chemistry Concoctions*. Charlotte turned from the charts and gave me a strange look. I gave her my best smile.

"Anne, keep an eye on Curious and the boys. Emily and I have a project to do for middle school," Charlotte said. She turned and walked up the stairs. Emily followed.

It was Anne's turn to make vegetable soup and cheese sandwiches. John Glenn and I were her assistants. Without Charlotte in the room, I wondered how Anne was going to keep everyone under control.

I kept *Cool Chemistry Concoctions* open, just in case I needed it for reference.

"How do you make soup into gold?" asked Anne.

"You can't turn soup into gold," Ben answered.

"You add twenty-four carrots!" Anne said and laughed.[36]

I watched as Anne got out the vegetables.

"Grab the lobster pot," she said. In this family, we make everything in vast amounts. Soup is made in a 100-quart lobster pot. Our pot has never held a lobster.

I grabbed the lobster pot.

The recipe called for sixteen cups of water. She poured water into a glass four-cup measure. I bent down to look to make sure the water level came exactly to the four-cup mark.

John Glenn looked up from the cereal-box tower he was building. "What are you doing?" he asked.

----

36   Technically, gold, which is a chemical element, is measured in karats not carrots. Carrots are orange, crunchy root vegetables. But I am sure you knew that.

"Checking the water level," I said. "My chemistry book says that you have to measure water at the bottom of the meniscus."[37]

----

37   A meniscus is the curved upper surface of a liquid in a test tube . . . or a measuring cup. And you might have noticed that cups are not SI units. But scientists sometimes have to work with whatever tools are available.

"This recipe doesn't call for a meniscus!"
Anne joked.

Anne is not a scientist. I pulled out a piece of Dad's graph paper. I drew a meniscus.[38]

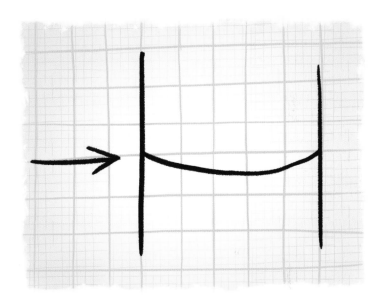

We dumped the water into the lobster pot.

We filled and dumped the four-cup measure a total of four times.[39]

----

38   Meniscus is from the Greek *menisci,* which means crescent. Crescent is a shape like a moon. It describes the curved surface of a liquid in a container.

39   Because 4 X 4 = 16 and the recipe called for 16 cups. I may be a slow reader, but I am really good at math!

"Next, we need sixteen cups of chicken stock," Anne said. "Do you measure chicken stock at the bottom of the meniscus too?"

I checked *Cool Chemistry Concoctions* and *Edible Chemicals*. They did not mention chicken stock.

Later that night, as we settled in for dinner, I thought about our team. Anne and I worked well together. Like cookies and milk.[40]

---

40   This is an analogy. An analogy compares things that are different from each other. Anne and I work well together, even if we aren't really cookies and milk. But John Glenn didn't do anything. So I guess he was kind of like asparagus, which does not go with cookies and milk.

13

Thursday, 3:45 p.m.

This was what I had been waiting for all week. When I got home from school, I was ready to make dinner. I would stay busy. Then Charlotte wouldn't notice that I didn't have a chore on the chore chart.

But Charlotte had been acting strange. Maybe she noticed already. I couldn't be sure.

I took a look at Dad's chart. I was careful to keep my eyes on the dinner chart. I did not dare glance at the chore chart.

Charlotte walked up next to me. Her eyes were on the chore chart. I tried to keep my breathing even. I tried not to blink.[41]

----

41   According to the FBI, which stands for Federal Bureau of Investigation, when you blink too much you might be guilty. Hopefully the FBI doesn't arrest people for avoiding chores.

Charlotte looked my way. I could feel her staring at me. I kept my eyes on the dinner chart. I wasn't really reading it. I was just pretending to read it. All my attention was on Charlotte. I braced myself.

"CURIOUS!" Charlotte shouted in my ear. "It is Thursday. It is your turn to make dinner."

I was relieved that she was yelling at me about the dinner chart and not the chore chart.

I put my finger on the dinner chart, tracing the line over from Thursday to the menu, even though I remembered that Dad had assigned me hot dogs and lemonade. My hand was shaking a little. I was hoping Charlotte did not know anything about FBI tricks to get people to confess.

Dad must not be too confident in my cooking. Hot dogs do not take much work. But I had something special planned. I was going to work on some mixtures. Then I would try my hand at dilution.[42]

---

42   Dilution is when you mix water into a solution to make it weaker. Like the way Mom and Dad always mix an extra can of water in with the orange juice.

I opened the refrigerator quickly so I could hide from Charlotte for a minute. I grabbed the ketchup, mustard, mayo, and lemons.

When I closed the refrigerator, Charlotte was gone.

John Glenn and Ben were my helpers. And of course, Edison stayed to watch. They had a wooden spoon, a spatula, and tongs. *Oh, great. The Three Musketeers.*[43]

Time for another hypothesis.

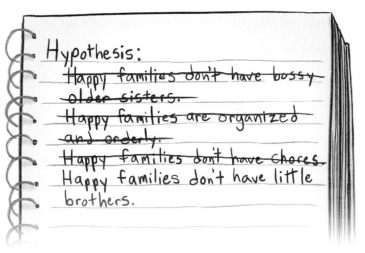

Hypothesis:
~~Happy families don't have bossy older sisters.~~
~~Happy families are organized and orderly.~~
~~Happy families don't have chores.~~
Happy families don't have little brothers.

---

43   *The Three Musketeers* is a book by Alexandre Dumas. The three guys that Alexandre Dumas wrote about probably had muskets and not kitchen utensils. And because I know that you are curious: YES, these are some of Ms. Fickleby's friends too.

I thought about ignoring my little brothers so I could focus more on chemistry and cooking.

But then I thought about it a little more. Emily and Anne had fun and still got dinner done. It might be interesting to see if John Glenn, Ben, and I had good family chemistry. We might have fun. Charlotte would never let me do what we were about to do.

I quickly ran to Dad's workshop. I grabbed four pairs of safety goggles. It wasn't really necessary, but I wanted it to feel like we were in a real laboratory.

Back in the kitchen, I grabbed some rubber gloves from under the sink. They were a little large and there were more left gloves than right. But remember, scientists have to work with what's available.

I got out the beakers. Beakers are used to measure liquids in chemistry class. We don't really have beakers. We were using the same measuring cups that Anne and I used yesterday. But a scientist has to know all the right terms.

My first experiment would be mixing the ketchup with the mustard.

"Why?" asked Edison.

"Just to see what will happen," I said.

"It'll turn orange," said Ben.

"Put on your goggles," I said, "and watch the experiment."

I knew that this wasn't a chemical reaction. It was a physical reaction. But I still wanted to try it.

I poured about 250 milliliters of ketchup into a bowl. Then I poured about 250 milliliters of mustard into the bowl.[44]

"Give me the wooden spoon," I said to John Glenn.

"No. I want to stir!" said John Glenn.

"No, me!" said Ben.

"ME!" shouted Edison.

"Let's take turns," I said, trying to gain some control over this team.

----

44   250 milliliters is almost exactly one cup.

I grabbed the spoon and stirred a couple of times.

"See?" said Ben. "Orange." I guess even kindergartners can do chemistry.

John Glenn stirred next. "Let's add something else," he said.

He grabbed a bottle of soy sauce.

"No one will want to eat that!" I shouted. This experiment was getting out of control. Before I could stop him, John Glenn dumped half the bottle into my mixture. I tried to grab it away from him before he could do more damage.

As I tried to pull the soy sauce away from him, I bumped into Ben. Ben stepped back and tipped over the chair that Edison was standing on. Edison grabbed for the cabinet knob to keep from falling. The cabinet swung open — Edison swinging along with it. His feet hit the bowl with the mustard mixture before he landed on the floor. The mixture splattered across the room. Another chain reaction.

"YUCK!" said Edison.

We stood still. We stared at the mess. Then a box of baking soda fell out of the cupboard and landed on the counter. I smiled.

Baking soda is a base. Ketchup and mustard contain vinegar. Vinegar is an acid. If you put an acid and base together, it will have a chemical reaction.[45]

I opened the baking soda box.

"What are you doing?" asked Ben.

"I am going to create a chemical reaction," I said.

"I want to try!" shouted John Glenn.

I started sprinkling baking soda over the mess. It started to fizz. It bubbled up. The mixture was growing and seemed to come alive.

"Cool!" said John Glenn as he took a spatula and started playing with the fizzing mixture on the floor. Ben and Edison laughed and joined him.

----

45 A chemical reaction is different from a physical reaction. In a physical reaction, the two substances don't change – they just mix together. Like ketchup and mustard. In a chemical reaction, a new substance is formed. And energy can be given off. It was a good thing we were wearing goggles!

"These bubbles are called carbon dioxide," I said.

"They are the same bubbles that are in soda pop."

"Maybe we can make soda pop!" said John Glenn.

I was sprinkling more baking soda when I heard
the back door open.

We looked at the door.

There stood Dad.

Home early.

In his nice clean suit.

He stared at the mess. We held our breath.

"At least you're wearing goggles," he said.

14

Thursday, 4:26 p.m.

I explained our experiment to Dad. He said, "Do you know what else is an acid?"

"Lemonade?" I said.

"No," he answered. "My homemade cleaner. It's made from vinegar too." He handed me the spray bottle. Then he went upstairs to change.

I was scrubbing the floor when Charlotte walked in. She just stared at me.

"I thought Emily was supposed to do the floors," she said. She hopped to the fridge around splattered mustardy globs. She looked at the chore chart. I practiced looking innocent. Looking innocent was pretty hard since I was cleaning a mustardy mess that I made myself.

"Hmm," said Charlotte. She glanced back at me one more time. Then she walked away.

I was sure she knew that I wasn't assigned a chore. I started to feel really guilty. But why wasn't she saying anything to Mom or Dad? Maybe she was waiting until she could get revenge.

Dad came back down the stairs. He said, "Let's finish the rest of this experiment together."

We mixed together ketchup and mayo. The ketchup plus mayo made a lighter red color. We already knew that because it was Mom's famous potato chip-dip recipe. She made it all the time. But all scientists know that an experiment should be repeatable.

Next we started on the lemonade.

Dad's lemonade recipe called for eight cups of water. We doubled it. Scientists don't use cups for measuring liquids. They use liters. But I didn't have much choice in the matter.[46]

Dad handed me the measuring cup. I poured the water into it and bent down. I had my face at the same height as the counter to look at the water level.

"Why?" asked Edison.

"You need to have your eyes at the same level as the water," Dad said, "so you can see the meniscus."

---

46   The United States is like Liberia and Myanmar, two other countries that don't use the SI or metric system. Scientists in the United States use SI units, but cooks in the United States like to stick to the old ways.

"Why?" asked Edison.

"So your measurement is accurate," I said, remembering yesterday's soup and the diagram in *Cool Chemistry*.

"Some liquids have a backward meniscus," Dad told Edison. "That's when it is higher in the middle than at the edges. You have to measure your liquid at the center of the meniscus."

I opened *Cool Chemistry* and showed the boys a diagram of a meniscus.

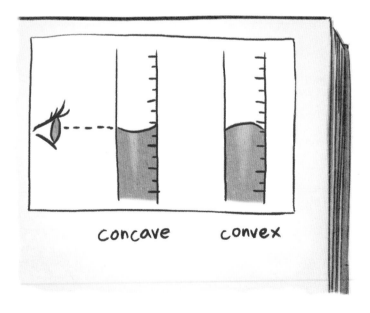

concave   convex

We added more water to the lemonade for good measure. This is called dilution.

Anne walked down the stairs. "Why did the lemon stop halfway across the road?" she asked.

"Lemons cannot walk," Ben said.

Anne rolled her eyes and said, "Because he ran out of juice!"

15

Friday, 1:15 p.m.

I was happy. It was almost the weekend. But what started out as a good day went terribly, terribly wrong. On my way to reading class with Ms. Fickleby, I ran into John Glenn in the hall.

"You'd better get back to your classroom. You don't want to get into trouble," I said to him.

He smiled and walked into Ms. Fickleby's class. "I have been promoted to the third-grade reading group."

My little second-grade brother with me in the same reading class! My life couldn't possibly be worse. I would never live this down.[47]

----

47   "Live this down" is an idiom. An idiom is a group of words that have a meaning that's not obvious from the actual words. "Live this down" means that this is something people will never forget. I knew that John Glenn would be sharing this story with the whole family. Forever. He would probably be telling his grandkids fifty years from now.

John Glenn walked to Ms. Fickleby's desk. He was probably batting his eyes. He was probably giving her his best smile.

"Oh my, aren't you charming?" she said. Every grown-up loves John Glenn. He smiled at me as he walked to his seat.

I could barely listen to Ms. Fickleby's directions. I was too horrified about John Glenn being in my class.

Ms. Fickleby handed out eighteen copies of *Little House on the Prairie*. I was too upset even to wonder whether Ms. Fickleby and Laura Ingalls went to the same one-room schoolhouse.[48]

"This book will be a challenge," said Ms. Fickleby. "But don't worry. I will read and you follow along."

I was starting to feel a little dizzy and knew I had to get it together. I focused on what I did best. Observation.

I observed Ms. Fickleby's lips as she read.

I observed Lin moving her finger across the page in her book.

I observed Henry handing Randy a note.

I observed the clock on the wall, its second hand moving slowly.

I observed John Glenn smirking and looking down at his book.

---

48   Okay. Not quite that upset. Laura Ingalls Wilder is the author of *Little House on the Prairie*. She was born in 1867. They probably didn't go to school together. But maybe Ms. Fickleby was her teacher.

I observed his book. His *UPSIDE-DOWN* book. John Glenn was not following along with Ms. Fickleby. Maybe John Glenn could *not* read at a third-grade level.

16

Friday, 3:45 p.m.

"Your parents are going to be a little late tonight," Aunt Dolly said. "The pizza dough is in the fridge, ready to go." She slipped out the back door so fast, no one had time to ask any questions.

I braced myself. Charlotte was reading the chore chart again. She was sure to notice my missing name, if she hadn't already. "We can skip homework tonight," said Charlotte. "It's Friday. Just do your chores," she said, looking right at me.

Suddenly Charlotte left the kitchen. Emily and Anne followed. I wondered if they were plotting revenge against me. Revenge for getting out of chores all week. Revenge that would probably involve a toilet brush. I had to do something about this mess.

I ran to look for Charlotte and saw Emily and Anne sitting in our room.

"Where's Charlotte?" I asked.

"*El baño!*" said Emily. "That means —"

"I know what it means," I said and rushed to the bathroom. There was Charlotte, looking at the toilet. She looked a little sick as she pulled on her gloves. I had to make things right.

"Charlotte?" I whispered.

"What?" she asked.

"If you mix baking soda with Dad's cleaner, it will bubble up and clean the toilet bowl. You won't have to scrub," I said.

"This toilet is disgusting," she said.

"I'll do it for you," I said. I figured that chemistry could happen in the bathroom too. But I didn't say that to Charlotte.

Charlotte smiled. "Yes. You will," she said. "Because you haven't done a chore all week."

She tried to hand me the brush, but I ran out of the room. I quickly grabbed the baking soda from the kitchen. The boys saw what I had grabbed and ran after me.

In the bathroom, the boys squeezed in behind me. Charlotte, Anne, and Emily squeezed in after the boys, wanting to know what we were up to.

"Wait!" shouted John Glenn. "I want to get some food coloring!"

"Good idea!" I said. John Glenn ran off.

Charlotte said, "This had better work, or you will be scrubbing toilets for me for the rest of the year."

When John Glenn came back, he put six drops of green food coloring into the toilet.

"You should have gotten yellow food coloring," said Ben.

"Ewwww."

"Gross."

"Yuck!"

Then I dumped in about 600 milliliters of vinegar.

"Nothing's happening," said Charlotte.

Then I dumped in some baking soda.

The mixture started to bubble up. Just like the mustard mixture yesterday.

It kept bubbling.

And bubbling.

And bubbling.

Right up to the rim.

"It's gonna blow!" shouted John Glenn. But just then the bubbles stopped. The mixture started to sink back into the toilet bowl.

"There," I said to Charlotte. "Now all you have to do is flush. No more scrubbing."

Friday, 4:45 p.m.

Later in the kitchen, John Glenn and Ben were ready to cook. Edison wanted to help. This was going to be interesting. And this was a good time to improve my hypothesis. I was pretty sure about this one:

Hypothesis:
~~Happy families don't have bossy older sisters.~~
~~Happy families are organized and orderly.~~
~~Happy families don't have chores.~~
~~Happy families don't have little brothers.~~
Happy families follow directions.

I settled in to observe.

John Glenn looked at Dad's instructions and new recipe. I doubted that he could read the big words, but I wasn't sure. He took out the pizza dough, the sauce, the plastic containers of pre-chopped toppings. He rolled out the dough into three big circles. They were not very symmetrical.[49]

----

49   Symmetrical means that one half is the mirror image of the other half. In other words, John Glenn's pizza crusts were not perfect circles. Whether symmetrical or not, three pizzas are probably not enough to feed seven kids.

At that point, Mom rushed in, setting down a load of books on the counter. "Sorry, Dad is going to be late, so I will help you with dinner." She looked at the pizza dough and said, "Those look interesting."

She turned on the oven. As John Glenn was covering each pizza crust with garlic sauce, Mom said, "Ben and Edison can help sprinkle the toppings." She slipped a file out from her pile of books and pulled out a sheet of music.

I observed Mom humming and singing with an occasional look up at the boys. She was practicing her songs for choir. John Glenn smirked as he spread the sauce over the top of each pizza.

"Not too much garlic sauce, John Glenn," Mom called. "I have choir practice tonight. I don't want to breathe garlic on my fellow singers. And I think we're out of mouthwash."

John Glenn stopped spreading garlic sauce and handed Ben a container of black olives. "Only put those on two pizzas," he said.

He handed Edison a container of onions. "Only put those on one pizza," he said.

John Glenn told the boys, "I have a secret ingredient." He took something out of the cupboard. He was turned away from me, so I could not see the secret ingredient.

18

Friday, 6:00 p.m.

Like clockwork, we shoved our way around the table.
Dad had returned and was pulling the pizzas out of
the oven.

"Huh, these don't smell like I expected," he said.

I glanced over at John Glenn. He was practicing
his angel look.

Dad and Mom dished out the pizzas. I saw little
white circles of chalky stuff on top.

I sniffed. Minty. I took a bite.

"YUCK!"

"EWWWW!!"

"GROSS!"

"JOHN GLENN MCCARTHY!" shouted Dad.
"What did you put on these pizzas?"

John Glenn looked startled. "I was being efficient!" he said. "Mom has choir practice tonight. She can't smell like garlic. I added breath mints!"

My brothers and sisters spit out their minty pizza. I looked at my parents, waiting for the scolding.

But Dad did not yell.

"You are right," he said. "We should all be more efficient. This was an interesting experiment."[50]

----

50   I wondered if this really was an experiment or John Glenn's grand plan to get out of kitchen duty for the next twelve years.

19

Friday, 7:16 p.m.

Eating out is a rare occasion when you are part of a big family. For one thing, it is expensive. For another, it is logistically challenging.[51]

But tonight, we made an exception. When Mom got back from choir practice, we went to Shakey's Pizza.

"This will be a reward for doing all your chores this week," Dad said.

Charlotte turned and looked at me. I shrunk down in my seat.

Since there are seven kids and two adults, dividing up pizzas that come in eight slices is a challenge.

---

51   Logistics are the things that must be done to plan a complicated activity that involves many people. Or just nine people, three of which are pesky little brothers.

As we debated the logistics, Dad ordered pitchers of water. That's another thing about big families — you get water. Nine different drinks is both expensive and confusing.

"Curious, why don't you choose one of the pizzas," Dad said. I was startled. I was being noticed. Maybe this was a trick.

"I want pepperoni," said Charlotte.

"Yuck!" said Edison.

"I want green olives and banana peppers, PORE-FUH-VOR!" said Emily.[52]

"Yuck! Yuck!" said Edison.

---

52 *Por favor* means "please." She's weird, but at least she has manners.

"I guess pepperoni would be okay," I said.
I was hoping to keep Charlotte from saying anything
about chores.[53]

We discussed the likelihood that Mom would
get whole-wheat crust and sauerkraut topping. The
waitress came back to the table with two pitchers
of water.

"MOOCHAS GRACIAS!" shouted Emily.
She exaggerated the *MOO* part. She's weird. The
waitress gave her a strange look and walked back
to the kitchen.

Dad pulled out his clipboard. He started to work
on a few equations. He was figuring how to divide up
the pizzas and to agree on the rest of the toppings.

He put the toppings in order from most liked
to least. Black olives and sausage were at the top
of the list. Goat cheese and sauerkraut were at
the bottom.

----
53   And besides, pepperoni is the most popular pizza topping in America. It would
probably keep Charlotte – and all the McCarthys – happy.

Dad finished his calculation. He announced, "In order for everyone to have an equal amount of pizza, we'll need to order nine pizzas. That's seventy-two slices, and we each get eight."

We all cheered.

"No," said Mom. The cheers died down.

"Fine," said Dad. "We will start with three pizzas. Each pizza is divided into eight pieces. We will cut one piece of each pizza in half for Ben and Edison."

We focused on choosing toppings. Then we focused on the drinks. Edison looked at the pitcher of water and said, "Look."

We all looked at the pitcher of water.

John Glenn asked, "Does soda pop have a meniscus?" He was probably hoping Dad would order a pitcher of pop. It didn't work.

Dad drew a meniscus on his clipboard.

He explained the curve on the surface of the liquid. He continued his explanation from yesterday's experiments.

He said, "A meniscus can either be concave or convex."[54]

"Wow," said John Glenn.

"Cool," said Ben.

"Yuck!" said Edison.

"What's in the water?" said the waitress as she approached our table again.

"A meniscus!" Edison shouted. We stared at him. It was probably the biggest word he'd ever said.

"Oh, I am so sorry! I will get you a new pitcher," said the waitress. She grabbed the pitcher of water and hustled back to the kitchen.

As my family giggled about the waitress's mistake, I asked Charlotte why she didn't tell on me.

"I get by on my wits," she said. "I am going to need your help sometime very soon."[55]

---

54   When a liquid curves inward, or down in a pitcher of water, it is concave. Convex is when the liquid curves outward, or up in a pitcher of water. It all depends on what atoms are in the liquid. But don't trust atoms – they make up everything.
55   I didn't know what Charlotte meant, but I suspected it involved chores. You'll just have to wait for another week in my life to find out.

I wondered what Charlotte had in store for me. And I wondered about this week of kitchen — and bathroom — experiments. And finally, I thought about what my hypothesis for the week should have been.

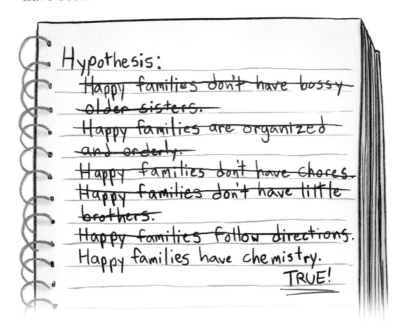

Hypothesis:
~~Happy families don't have bossy older sisters.~~
~~Happy families are organized and orderly.~~
~~Happy families don't have chores.~~
~~Happy families don't have little brothers.~~
~~Happy families follow directions.~~
Happy families have chemistry.
TRUE!

The problem is, a scientist is supposed to make the hypothesis before the experiment. Not at the end. Hypotheses — and families — are a lot of work.

Conclusions

Scientists like to make conclusions. And my main conclusion is that all happy families are not alike. Some families are messy. But having family chemistry can help. Here are more conclusions for this week:

- Charts can be helpful to scientists.

- The waitress is not a scientist.

- Always eat sliquid with a spork.

- I got out of doing chores.[56]

- Dad forgot to change out of his suit.

---

56   But in case you didn't notice, Charlotte got out of being a team helper. She will never play second fiddle to anyone. "Playing second fiddle," by the way, is another idiom. And if you don't remember what an idiom is, you need to go back to Chapter 15. "Playing second fiddle," is something Charlotte can't do, because she is bossy.

SCIENCE STUNT
HOW TO CLEAN A TOILET

You'll want to do this chore at least once a week. It is fun. No kidding. Try it.

What you need:

- a toilet
- a measuring cup
- vinegar
- baking soda

What you do:

1. Measure about 1 cup of vinegar. Pour it into the toilet bowl.
2. Measure about 1 cup of baking soda. Pour it into the toilet.
3. Watch it fizzle and bubble.
4. When it's all done bubbling, flush it down!
5. Go find an adult and collect your allowance.

For more fun science stunts, visit: www.torychristie.com

🦢 GLOSSARY 🦢

ancient (AYN-shuhnt)–very old

chaos (KAY-oss)–total confusion

chemical reaction (KEM-uh-kuhl ree-AK-shuhn)–a process in which one or more substances are changed to one or more different substances

chemist (KEM-ist)–a person trained in the scientific study of substances, what they are composed of, and how they react with each other

engineer (en-juh-NEAR)–someone who is trained to design and build machines, vehicles, bridges, roads, or other structures

environmentally responsible (en-VYE-ruhn-men-tuh-lee ri-SPON-suh-buhl)–referring to actions that protect or help the environment

hypothesis (hye-POTH-uh-siss)–a prediction that can be tested about how a scientific investigation or experiment will turn out

logistics (loh-JIS-tiks)–the detailed planning of a complex operation or event involving many people or supplies

mixture (MIKS-chur)–two or more substances that are mixed together but not chemically combined

observe (uhb-ZURV)–to watch someone or something carefully

precise (pri-SISE)–in science, the closeness of two or more measurements

professor (pruh-FESS-ur)–a teacher of the highest teaching rank at a college or university

scientific method (sye-uhn-TIF-ik METH-uhd)–the rules and procedures in science involving the finding and stating of a problem, the collection of facts through observation and experiment, and the making and testing of ideas that need to be proven right or wrong

solution (suh-LOO-shuhn)–a mixture made up of a substance that has been dissolved in a liquid

FURTHER INQUIRIES

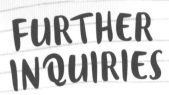

1. Explain why Curious didn't tell anyone she wasn't assigned a chore. Were her reasons good ones?

2. If you were in Curious's situation, would you confess that you weren't assigned a chore?

3. Do you think Curious has the traits to be a good scientist? Explain your answer with examples from the text.

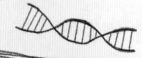

RECORD YOUR FINDINGS

1. Curious includes several charts in this book. Create a chart of your own that shows your daily schedule.

2. On page 40, Curious lists both Ms. Fickleby's and her own book rules. What are your top five book rules?

3. Curious had several hypotheses about happy families. Write your own happy-family hypothesis and explain why it is true.

REFERENCES

Scientists should tell readers where they got their information. We call these "References." Scientists do this in case readers want to do more research.

MRS. MCCARTHY'S AND MS. FICKLEBY'S REFERENCE LIST

Rapunzel: Her Princess Journal[1] by Rapunzel

Frankenstein by Mary Shelley

Little House on the Prairie by Laura Ingalls Wilder

Gift of Peace: The Jimmy Carter Story by Elizabeth Raum

Mixtures and Solutions by Hugh Westrup

Cool Chemistry Concoctions by Covay Lent Bond[2]

Edible Chemicals by Tory Christie[3]

Original Recipe by Jessica Young

In the Night Kitchen by Maurice Sendak

1   I just made this up. This is fiction, remember?
2   I made this up too.
3   I made this up but it sounds like a fun book to write.

ABOUT THE AUTHOR

Tory Christie is a real scientist by day and secretly writes children's books at night. When it is light outside, she studies rocks and water. After dark, she writes silly science stories that kids and grown-ups can laugh about. Although she grew up in a large family, her family was nothing like the McCarthys — honestly. The McCarthys are completely fictional — really. Tory Christie lives in Fargo, North Dakota, with her medium-sized family.

ABOUT THE ILLUSTRATOR

As a professional illustrator and designer, Mina Price has a particular love for book illustration and character design, or basically any project that allows her to draw interesting people in cool outfits. Mina graduated from the Maryland Institute College of Art with a BFA in Illustration. When she is not drawing, Mina can frequently be found baking things with lots of sugar or getting way too emotional over a good book.

MAKE MORE DISCOVERIES WITH CURIOUS!

FIND:

Videos & Contests
Games & Puzzles
Heroes & Villains
Authors & Illustrators

www.CAPSTONEKIDS.com

Find cool websites and more books just like this one at
www.FACTHOUND.com. Just type in the book I.D.
9781515816461 and you're ready to go!